The PEDDLER and the BAKER

To my father, who read to me.
YM

To Ora Eitan, my teacher, my mentor, my friend.
LG

Green
Bean
Books

First published in the UK in 2020 by Green Bean Books
c/o Pen & Sword Books Ltd
47 Church Street, Barnsley, S. Yorkshire, S70 2AS
www.greenbeanbooks.com

Paperback edition: 978-1-78438-481-4
Harold Grinspoon Foundation edition: 978-1-78438-485-2

Designed by Tina Garcia
Edited by Kate Baker and Julie Carpenter
Production by Hugh Allan

Printed in China by Printworks Global Ltd, London and Hong Kong
CIP Code 042033.8K1/B1066/A7

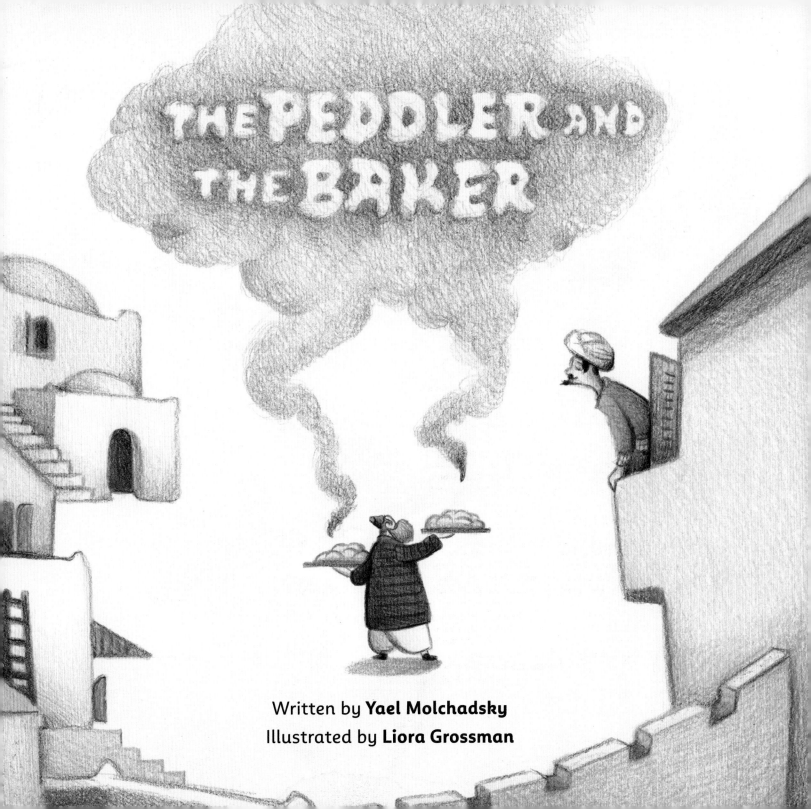

THE PEDDLER AND THE BAKER

Written by **Yael Molchadsky**

Illustrated by **Liora Grossman**

Long ago, in an old city surrounded by walls, there lived a poor peddler.

Every day, he would wake up at the crack of dawn and set out to sell his goods from door to door. His meagre earnings were barely enough to buy a little food and pay the rent, but the peddler was happy with what he had.

From his tiny room above a bakery, he could
catch the delicious scent of freshly-baked bread.
Every morning, he would open his window and
sing merrily, "Hurray for a new day and for the
delicious smell that floats my way."

But one morning, when the baker heard the
peddler's song, he flew into a rage.
"Get your nose away from that window!"
the baker yelled at him.
"I work hard to knead the dough, I fire up the oven
and bake the bread, and you? You just
stand there and enjoy my work for free!"

The poor peddler heard the booming voice of the
baker and quickly ducked back inside his room.

On the following day, an errand boy climbed to the peddler's attic with a message. "The rabbi wants you to come to his house straight away," he told him. The peddler happily followed the boy, wondering why he had been summoned. Perhaps the rabbi needed his help?

But when he arrived at the rabbi's house, his heart sank. Inside he could hear the angry voice of the baker complaining, "Every morning this cunning peddler enjoys the precious smell of my bread for free. Don't I deserve payment for my work?"

When, at last, the peddler plucked up the courage to knock on the door, the rabbi greeted him soberly. "I hear that every day you enjoy the smell of freshly-baked bread without paying a penny," he said.

"To repay your debt to the baker," the rabbi continued, "you will have to work extra hard all week long. On Friday morning you must return to my house with the coins you have earned. The baker and I will be waiting for you."

The baker smiled and rubbed his hands together with glee. Finally, he would get what he was owed!

That week, the peddler worked harder than ever. He woke up before daybreak and walked from market to market and street to street to sell his wares. He wandered to every corner of the city and returned to his room late at night.

On Friday morning, the peddler counted his earnings.
He had managed to earn a few more coins than
usual. He kept one coin to buy a little food for
Shabbat, tied the rest in a small cloth pouch, and
set out for the rabbi's house.

"I hope you saved up a lot of coins," sneered
the baker, who was already waiting for him.
"You owe me plenty for the delicious smell of
my bread."

The peddler kept his head down in silence and
handed the pouch to the rabbi.

The rabbi accepted the pouch and shook it
firmly – up and down, side to side. The coins
danced inside it, jingling like golden bells.
Then he turned to the baker and said, "There are
a lot of coins in this purse. Did you hear them ring?
Did it please your ears?"

The baker nodded impatiently. He reached for the pouch as the rabbi continued, "If so, then the sound of the coins will be your payment for the smell of the bread."

The baker's hand dropped down silently, and a gentle smile spread over the peddler's face.

"Many wonderful things are given in this world for free, such as sweet scents and beautiful sounds," said the rabbi. "Soon it will be Shabbat – a day of rest. This special day was also given to us for free, a beautiful gift for everyone – young and old, rich and poor, man and animal alike."

On his way home, the peddler used his hard-earned money
to buy two freshly-baked challot for Shabbat. "A special day,"
he thought. He knew that tonight he would finally enjoy both
their delectable smell *and* their delicious taste – a double delight!

Challah

Ingredients for the dough

600g (5 cups) plain/all-purpose flour

1 teaspoon salt

65g (¹/₃ cup) sugar

4 teaspoons dry yeast

3 tablespoons soft butter or oil

1 large egg

300ml (1¼ cups) warm water

Ingredients for the glaze

1 egg yolk, beaten with 1 tablespoon water

90g (½ cup) sesame seeds or poppy seeds

Instructions

1. Place all ingredients in a large bowl: flour, salt, sugar, yeast, butter, egg, and water. Mix until the dough is smooth.

2. Knead well on a floured surface for 10 minutes. If the dough is still sticky, add a little more flour.

3. Roll the dough into a ball and place in a lightly oiled bowl. Cover with a towel, and let the dough rise for 60–90 minutes, until the dough doubles in size.

4. After the dough has risen, remove from the bowl and knead a bit more. Divide the dough into three equal pieces. Roll each piece into a long, thin rope. Connect all three ropes at the top and braid. Pinch the end of the braid and fold underneath the edge of the challah.

5. Place the braided challah on a baking tray lined with baking paper. Cover with a towel and let it rise for another 40–45 minutes, until the challah has doubled in size.

6. Dip a pastry brush into the beaten egg yolk and water, and brush the challah with the glaze.

7. Sprinkle sesame or poppy seeds on top of the challah. Place the pan in a pre-heated oven (180C / 350F) and bake for 45 minutes or until the challah turns golden.

8. Take the challah out of the oven and let it cool on a baking rack.

9. Enjoy smelling *and* eating your delicious challah!